Wherever You Are

my love will find you

Nancy Tillman

FEIWEL AND FRIENDS

NEW YORK

I wanted you more
than you ever will know,
so I sent love to follow
wherever you go.

It's high as you wish it. It's quick as an elf.
You'll never outgrow it…it stretches itself!

So climb any mountain . . .
climb up to the sky!
My love will find you.
My love can fly!

Make a big splash! Go out on a limb!
My love will find you. My love can swim!

It never gets lost, never fades, never ends . . .

if you're working . . .

or playing . . .

or sitting with friends.

You can dance 'til you're dizzy...

paint 'til you're blue....

There's no place, not one,
that my love can't find you.

And if someday you're lonely,
or someday you're sad,
or you strike out at baseball,
or think you've been bad...

just lift up your face, feel the wind in your hair.
That's me, my sweet baby, my love is right there.

In the green of the grass ... in the smell of
the sea ... in the clouds floating by ...
at the top of a tree ... in the sound
crickets make at the end of the day ...

"You are loved. You are loved. You are
loved," they all say.

My love is so high, and so wide and so deep, it's always right there, even when you're asleep.

So hold your head high
and don't be afraid
to march to the front
of your own parade.

If you're still my small babe
or you're all the way grown,
my promise to you
is you're never alone.

You are my angel, my darling,
my star . . . and my love will find you,
wherever you are.

To Daddy, whose love always finds me, wherever I am.

A FEIWEL AND FRIENDS BOOK
An Imprint of Macmillan

WHEREVER YOU ARE. Copyright © 2010 by Nancy Tillman. All rights reserved.
Printed in the United States of America by Lehigh Phoenix, Rockaway, New Jersey.
For information, address Feiwel and Friends, 175 Fifth Avenue, New York, N.Y. 10010.

Library of Congress Cataloging-in-Publication Data Available

ISBN: 978-0-312-54966-4

Book design by Nancy Tillman and Kathleen Breitenfeld

Feiwel and Friends logo designed by Filomena Tuosto

First Edition: 2010

10 9 8

mackids.com

You are loved.